Touch! Touch!

by Riki Levinson
pictures by True Kelley

E. P. DUTTON · NEW YORK

Library of Congress Cataloging in Publication Data

Levinson, Riki.   Touch! Touch!

Summary: A toddler creates pandemonium as he
touches everyone in the house, including the bird in its cage.
[1. Humorous stories]   I. Kelley, True, ill.   II. Title.
PZ7.L5796To   1987   [E]   86-29056
ISBN 0-525-44309-6

Published in the United States by E. P. Dutton,
2 Park Avenue, New York, N.Y. 10016

Published simultaneously in Canada by
Fitzhenry & Whiteside Limited, Toronto

Editor: Ann Durell   Designer: Riki Levinson

Printed in Hong Kong by South China Printing Co.
First Edition   COBE   10 9 8 7 6 5 4 3 2 1

91 - 7211

to Gerry, I do remember
R.L.

for Jada Lindblom
T.K.

"Touch cat."

"Touch dog."

"Touch sister."

"Touch brother."

"Touch baby."

"Touch bird."

"Mama! Mama!"

"Fly!"

"Fly!"

"Touch sky!"

E
L

Levinson, Riki.

Touch! Touch!

HAWTHORNE ELEMENTARY SCHOOL
HAWTHORNE NEW YORK